TRIXIE TEMPEST'S DIARY

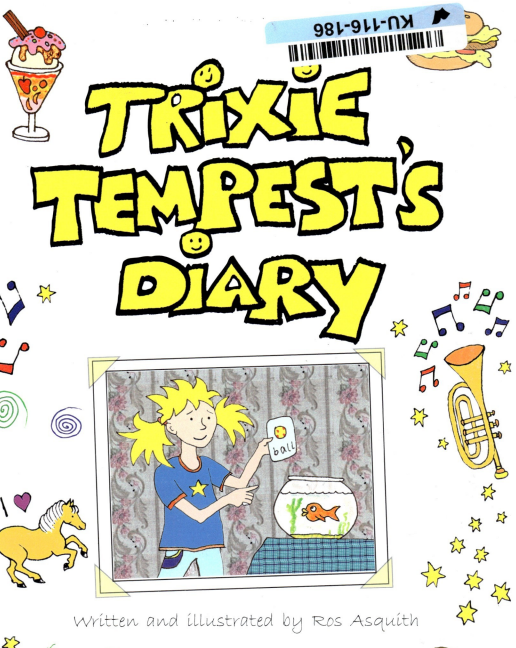

Written and illustrated by Ros Asquith

Collins

VERY EXTREMELY BORING DIARY
YOU'RE WELCOME TO READ IT

Hah! I've called this diary BORING to stop nosey parkers trying to get their hands on it.

Trixie's tip: Never write **"TOP SECRET"** or **"PARENTS KEEP OUT"** because everyone will try to have a peek.

2

ABOUT ME

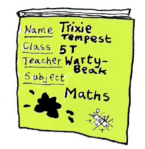

Name: Trixie Tempest

School: St Aubergine's Primary

Hair: Straw mat. I keep it in bunches. I did it up in beads once for World Bead Day or something, but they all fell out in assembly. Ping ping pingetty ping.

Teeth: One stupid baby tooth in front, which looks like a polar bear cub standing among a lot of icebergs.

Face: Freckles with bits of skin in-between. Thank goodness for skin, I say. Without it, we'd all fall out.

Size: I'm the smallest and thinnest in my class so I look like a twig in a jungle.

Family: I've got two whole parents both living at home, which means, as my Granny Clump is always telling me, that I'm Very Extremely lucky and should never complain about anything.

Mum is a teacher, but a very nice one. I wish she was my teacher instead of Warty-Beak, our miserable class teacher.

Warty-Beak in a happy mood

Dad is a builder. He either has too many jobs so we never see him or no jobs at all so he's getting under Mum's feet and not making any money.

Tomato is my little brother, age four. He's Very Extremely round and Very Extremely red. I've no idea how he got to be called Tomato.

Grannies: **Granny Clump** is kind, cosy and tries to make me eat more. **Granny Tempest** is exciting, wears purple jump suits and drives a flashy car.

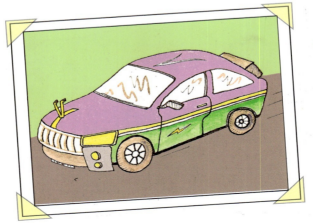

Vroom Vroom

5

Best friends: Chloe Caution is small and nervous. She's Very Extremely shy and a goody-goody. She's also a brainiac. She always carries Anty, her pet ant, everywhere in a matchbox as well as at least four bags of sweeties, which she hides up her jumper.

Chloe Caution

Dinah Dare de-Ville

Dinah Dare de-Ville is tall, brave and Very Extremely naughty. She'll be an actor or a ventriloquist when she grows up. She can imitate anyone's voice, even our demon teacher, Warty-Beak.

Boy friends: You know, friends who are boys. **Dennis** and **Sumil** are in my class. They're good fun and not bossy and bullying like some of the other boys.

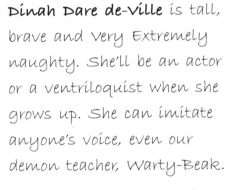

Dennis and Sumil

Pets: **Harpo**, our dog. Mum and Dad found her abandoned in a park with a "Not wanted" sign round her neck. She was all starved and manky, like a used teabag. But she soon changed into a cuddly pillow. THEN she had five puppies. We gave four of the puppies to kind homes, but I couldn't bear to part with bouncy **Bonzo**. He loves me best too and sleeps on my bed every night.

Harpo

Bonzo

Merlin, my palomino stallion (that's a gold-coloured boy horse, in case you didn't know). I haven't actually got Merlin as yet, but I'm saving every spare penny so I can fulfil my dream to buy him.

Hobbies: **Music:** I love to play the trumpet even though I'm not supposed to 'cos of my baby tooth. **Horses:** But I've only ever been horse riding four times because Mum says we're not made of money.

Politics (yes, children can get involved):

Animal rights: Animals are people too. Nicer than us, in fact. I once campaigned for human rights for nits. I thought they looked sweet with their little squashy bodies and cute wiggly legs.

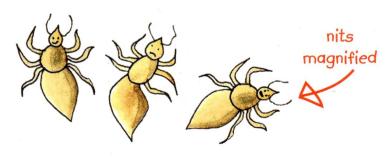

nits magnified

But I discovered that nits do in actual fact suck human blood, which makes them more like vamp. than animals. So I've crossed them off my list of animals to help. For last term's project, I did a brilliant animal magazine, which even impressed grumpy Warty-Beak.

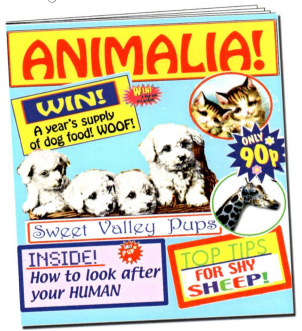

The environment: Did you know that a whole acre of rainforest is disappearing every second? That's bigger than our school playground.
It's disgustrous that we're shaving off rainforest as though it was some old moustache.

Favourite food: Meringues and roast potatoes. And, sorry, vegetables. I'm a vegetarian. Granny Clump said, "You won't grow big and strong without eating meat," so I said, "Look at gorillas."

Other favourite stuff: Too much to mention so HERE IS A PICTURE OF MY BRAIN, so you can see at a glance everything that's in it:

Ambitions: To be a world-famous trumpet player, horse rider and first child president of the world, when I'll arrange ice-cream vans, adventure playgrounds and discos on every street corner. I hope to achieve most of these ambitions by next year.

FOOTBALL 3:00!

SUNDAY

Aha! I start the brand new page of this fantastic diary. I'm going to write in it EVERY DAY.

Some people keep diaries on the net as blogs, but I prefer writing like this because:

a) I don't want the whole wide world reading it.

b) I can doodle like this:

or write in *nice flowing pink, like this,*

or BIG SCRATCHY BROWN, LIKE THIS,

or *olde worlde blue, like this,*

or pretty rainbow like this,

or stick things in, like this:

To: Darling Trisca Happy Birthday All my love & Hugs xx Granny Chirp xx xx

LUCKY 5P

11

Midnight

Not asleep. Tomato has just come into my room after dreaming he fell down the loo. I told him he was too round to fit down the loo but he's decided to sleep in my bed anyway, just to make sure.

1:00 a.m.

Still not asleep. It's very hot in my bed, with Harpo, Bonzo and Tomato.

MONDAY

If only school looked like this! ↙

Tired, but had to go to school. St Aubergine's Primary looks like a squashed egg carton. Why can't I go to a proper school with turrets and talking portraits?

I was just doing some fancy doodles of Merlin, when the laser eyes of Warty-Beak fell upon me.

"Have you been listening, Patricia?" he croaked. Warty-Beak sounds like a walrus gargling cement. And he always calls me by my full name, which I HATE.

"Oh yes, Sir," I replied. Not really. I just stared at Warty dumbly. It turned out Warty was setting us a PROJECT, and for once we could choose our own! "So I could do animal rights, or the environment?" I squeaked.

13

"I suppose so," said Warty, "as long as you remember that nature is red in tooth and claw, and that my pet, a snake, has the right to eat cuddly little mice."

"Guess what?" I said to Dinah and Chloe at break. "I'm going to teach Bonzo to read."

"Don't be daft!" said Dinah. "You tried that before, remember? You did a whole magazine for animals, and Bonzo couldn't read a word."

"Yeah, yeah, well, I didn't have enough time to teach him then. Chimps can do sign language. Dogs understand stuff like 'sit' and 'walkies', which is a lot more than human babies understand, so why shouldn't they learn more? It's only 'cos we never bother to teach animals anything that people think they're dumb."

Chloe and Dinah groaned. Humph. Nobody understands.

4:30 p.m.

Got home to find a disgustrous smell in the house. The kitchen had been taken over by Tomato and his little fiends from nursery. They were making a potion out of rotten eggs and washing-up liquid.

Upstairs, I perched on my bed trying to get some peace and quiet to think about my project.

TUESDAY

School. Nothing to report.

6:00 p.m.

Someone has eaten my tea. I left the table for two seconds to make a Very Extremely important emergency phone call to Dinah and when I got back my plate was empty.

"It was Bonzo," said Tomato, but I noticed he was looking rounder and redder than ever. In fact, he was looking like a person who'd eaten two suppers.

"Mum! He's eaten my tea!" I wailed in my best tragic wailing way.

But Mum believed Tomato. That's what life's like when you're the oldest.

16

7:00 p.m.

Spent two hours showing Bonzo flash cards with really simple words and pictures, like you do with little kids. One said "ball" and one said "cat".

Trouble is, Bonzo couldn't say the words, and so it was hard to know if he understood or not. I went to make myself a banana milkshake.

When I got back upstairs, Bonzo had chewed up my lovely flash cards.

"Why did you do that, Bonzo?" But he just wagged his tail.

9:00 p.m.

Writing this on bed with Harpo and Bonzo curled up on top of me. At least it's warm.

WEDNESDAY

5:00 p.m.

I tried the flash cards on next-door-but-one's goldfish, who just swam about. I tried to get it to wave its fins when it saw "ball" but I don't think it could hear me properly through the bowl.

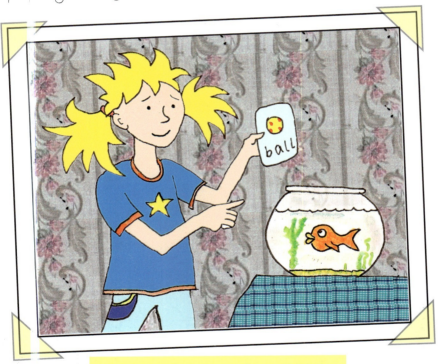

next-door-but-one's goldfish

Had a go with the hamster over the road, but it just ran about on its wheel like a furry blur.

the hamster over the road

Tried with next-door's cat, who just yawned.
It didn't even seem to notice the picture of a cat, which I'd have thought might make it purr or wave its tail about.

next-door's cat

19

9:00 p.m.

V.V.V. TIRED. I've just written a fantastic essay about how animals are as good as, or better than, humans in every way. I know this will impress even Warty-Beak. I spiced it up with a nice little diary entry, showing how good-natured dogs are, to prove they're better than us.

DOGGY DIARY

7:00 a.m. Whooppeee. Humans coming downstairs! Wag wag wagetty wag.

7:30 a.m. Breakfast! The best! Lick lick licketty lick.

8:30 a.m. Yes! Out for a wee wee. Fantastic! Wag wag wagetty wag.

8:45 a.m. Postman! Yeah! Woof woof woofetty woof.

9:00 a.m. Hurrah! A drink of lovely water! Wag wag slurp.

10:00 a.m. A little roll! And a nap! Lovely!

11:00 a.m. Play with my ball! Fantastic!
And so it goes on all day ... until ...

5:00 p.m. Family home! Amazing! Who do I
love most? All of them! Wag wag wag.
Lick lick lick. Bounce bounce bounce.

6:00 p.m. Hey! Lucky me! I'm going for a walk!
Wooferama!

7:00 p.m. Food! Too much happiness!
Wag wag snooze.

There. I think I've proved my point.

THURSDAY

I asked Chloe a big favour on the way home from school. "Could I borrow Anty, just for one night?"

"Why?" asked Chloe, very anxiously.

"Well, he's a Very Extremely special ant and I just want to see if I can prove he's better than all the others. It's for my project."

Chloe is very proud of Anty, so she was quite keen to find out if he had a large brain. Also, she is Very Extremely kind and never says no to anything, so she gave me Anty in his matchbox and told me to look after him. Then she gave me a recipe for his dinner!

Ingredients:

one egg

about three tablespoons of honey

gelatine

one multi-vitamin capsule

300–500 millilitres of cold water

Help! I didn't know I had to cook for Anty.

7:00 p.m.

A bad thing has happened. I had it all worked out.
I did, really. I cooked Anty's supper and put it in the
fridge to set. How ridiculous. As Mum said, I could
have given him a nibble of fruit. Or a bit of insect.
Or some ham.

BUT ... when I went to get him out for my intelligence test (I had it all worked out), he'd escaped! There was a teeny gap in the matchbox. I must have left it open when I checked on him and Anty, who is no fool, had seen his chance. How will I tell Chloe?

Mum found me crying and clutching the empty matchbox. She was very kind and said not to worry, I wouldn't have to tell Chloe.

"What do you mean, I'll have to go to a new school and never see my bestest friend in all the world EVER again?" I sobbed.

"Just get another ant," said Mum.

9:00 p.m.

It's quite hard catching an ant after dark, but I think I've found one very like Anty. If Chloe realises it's not him, I will be alone and friendless.

So now I've failed to teach anything to dogs, hamsters, goldfish, cats ... and ants. I think I'll have to find a talking animal, like a parrot.

25

Midnight

Woken by horrible wheezing sound.

Eeek. A ghost? Crept out of bed shaking like a leaf.
Looked under bed. Nothing under bed. Looked in
cupboard. Nothing in cupboard. No ghost.

Wheezy, creaky sound getting worse.

Tiptoed to door. Did I dare open it?

I decided to beat the ghost at its own game and scare it back, so I flung open the door and shrieked. Silence.

WHEEZE
WHEEZE
WHEEZE

The wheezing had gone! It was replaced by groans and curses from my parents' room, as in, "What's that horrible racket?"

"Sorry, bad dream," I squeaked.

Crept back to bed.

WHEEZE

2:00 a.m.

The wheezing again! Really close! Couldn't stop myself. Screamed Very Extremely loudly. My door burst open and a flapping white figure staggered in groaning. I screamed a lot louder.

It was Dad, dressed in Mum's long frilly summer dressing gown, which he'd obviously pulled on by mistake in the dark.

I explained.

We listened.

"Really loud?" he said.

WHEEZE
WHEEZE
WHEEZE

"REALLY loud," I said. But we couldn't hear a thing.

Just as Dad turned to go, it started again, right near the bed. No. On the bed.

"It's Bonzo," said Dad, looking worried. "I don't like the sound of that."

FRIDAY

I asked Mum if I could stay home from school to look after Bonzo. She said, "No." A bad day.

a) I'm Very Extremely worried about Bonzo. Mum said she'd take him to the vet if the wheeze hasn't improved.

b) At school, Warty-Beak wasn't a bit impressed with my fantastic essay. I showed it to Dinah and Chloe and even they seem to think I'm barking up the wrong tree, so to speak. At least Chloe welcomed Anty 2 as if he were her own.

ANTY!

c) It was raining, which meant wet play.
Football cancelled.

4:30 p.m.

Got home to find Bonzo still poorly. Mum said she thought he'd be fine, but his nose is dry. (If you're not a doggy person you may find this rather an odd remark, as most of us want our noses to be dry. But a dog's nose should be damp – so don't say this diary's not teaching you anything.)

Happy person DRY nose

Happy dog WET nose

"You shouldn't have made me go to school today. Animals don't have to go to school," I said, cuddling Bonzo.

"No, but they have to live out in the cold and wet and be in fear of their lives in case something comes to eat them. And all they think about is food," said Mum.

Hmmm. That's very true. Whenever you see a cow, it's eating.

No I'm not

32

munch, munch.   munch

"Would you want to curl up in a basket all day and eat out of a bowl?" said Mum.

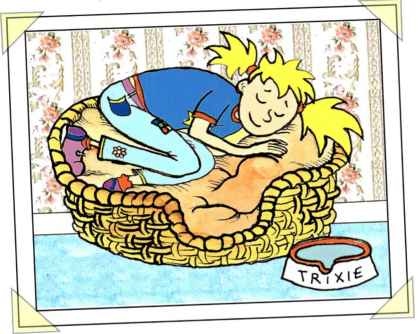

I didn't say yes, but that got me thinking about school, and how it could be so fantastic that I'd never want a day off – ever!

6:00 p.m.

Here's my plan for the perfect school. Make sure everyone learns to read, write and count to 20.

Outside, instead of the usual slab of concrete that we have to play in whether we like it or not, there'd be:

- an adventure playground
- a football pitch
- a vegetable garden
- an animal farm
- a pond.

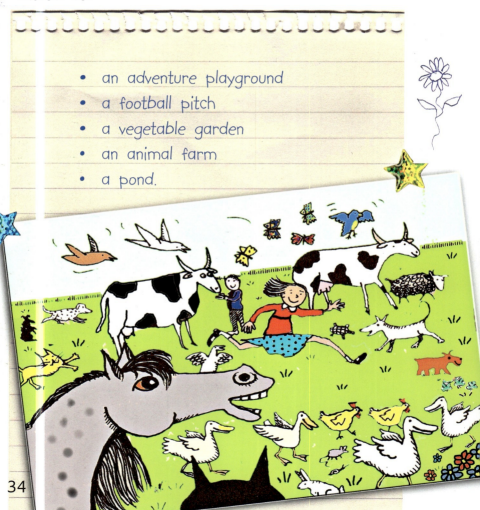

VEGETABLE GARDEN

POND

Inside there should be loads of special comfy areas,
a bit like in playgroup, for FREE TIME.
These would include:

- an edible castle
- a book room full of real stories and encyclopaedias about space and adventures
- a dressing-up tent
- a cookery room
- a room packed full of musical instruments
- a big art studio
- a proper theatre with a stage.

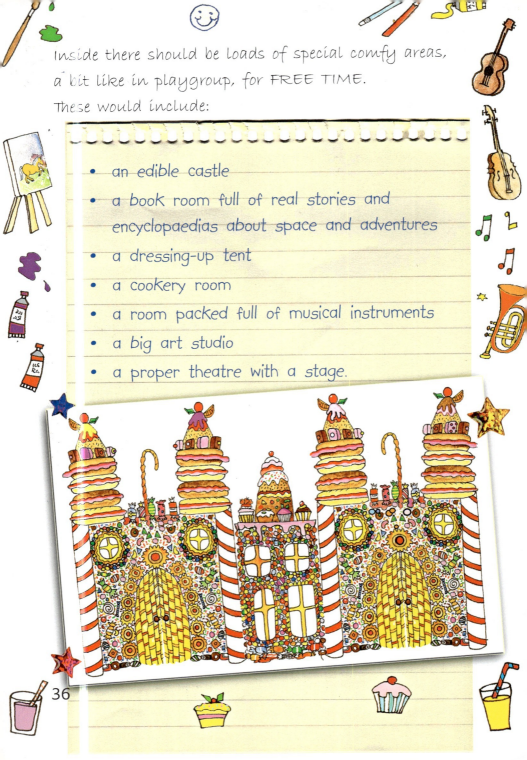

The walls would be covered with sweetie recipes, interesting maps that show you stuff about planets and parrots, interesting facts like who invented the potato chip and whether it's true that football was started by someone kicking an enemy's severed head.

2:00 a.m.

Bonzo was wheezing again. And he was sick. Woke Mum. Bad idea.

"We can't ring the vet now. Puppies are often sick."

Nobody cares.

SATURDAY

Me, Dinah and Chloe went round to Sumil's house to teach his parrot to read.

"This is a ball, Sinbad," I said, showing the parrot my first flash card. "Can you say 'ball'?"

"Ball!" he squawked, immediately.

"He's just parrot-ing," said Sumil.

"OK, what's this?" I asked, and I held up a cow.

"Cow!" he screeched.

"And this?"

"Fish!" he squawked.

I was really excited. "He knows! He knows!"

"Oh Trixie, don't be daft," said Chloe, "it's Dinah."

Sure enough, Dinah, who can copy any voice in the world, was on the floor having a monstrous giggling fit.

Ho! Heh! Ha Ha

Ha Ha Ho Ho
giggle giggle

I can take a joke, of course.

Now I'd failed with dogs, cats, fish, hamsters, ants AND parrots.

4:00 p.m.

Dinah bought me a strawberry cornet on the way home to make up and insisted my project would still work, because Chloe had a great idea.

I wasn't in the mood to hear it, but I must admit it was brilliant.

We're going to make a radio show for animals, because if they can't read, they can certainly hear! I'm going to do fake interviews and Dinah, with her very Extremely brilliant mimicking skills, will do all the voices. YES!

SUNDAY

Spent all day making a fake radio programme. We used Dinah's sister's minidisc. It's brilliant.

We've got Mrs Cluck the hen, complaining about the way she's kept in a horrid little cage and all her babies are taken from her. Dinah was very convincing as Mrs Cluck. Mum came barging in thinking we'd kidnapped a chicken farm. Me and Chloe did a heartbreaking chorus of baby chicks and Mum gave us a lecture about how the eggs you eat don't actually have chicks in.

Dinah was very good at Mrs Moo (the cow, obviously, I'll think of better names for the final tape), who mooed on about being milked too often and being treated no better than a cow (heh heh).

We also did a very tragic scene of a dog, Wuffles, who'd been abandoned as a puppy.

We ended on a happy note with all the animals singing a song. Me and Chloe did a harmony of neighs and whinnies and bleats. The chorus was:

We were all going out of our MINDS
Until somebody treated us KIND.
So always remember, whatever you do,
That ANIMALS ARE PEOPLE TOO!

I bet we could win a talent show as a trio, maybe calling ourselves The Bleatles. No one else at school will have anything like it.

9.00: p.m.

A terrible thing happened. Bonzo's wheeze got worse and he's been Very Extremely sick. Seven times!

1.
2.
3.
4.
5.
6.
7.

Mum rang the animal hospital emergency line. Now we're sitting in the animal hospital with Bonzo all tucked up in his blanket looking as if he's breathing his last.

1:00 a.m.

We had to leave Bonzo at the hospital. I begged and begged to stay the night with him, but the vet wouldn't let me. She looks quite fierce and I think Bonzo is frightened of her. She said, "If he makes it through the night, he should be fine."

If he makes it through the night! How does she expect me to sleep? How will I live without Bonzo?

I can't believe I've been worrying about stupid fake animal interviews when Bonzo, my REAL pet and king of my heart, is at death's door!

2:00 a.m.

Harpo is snoring on my bed as if she hasn't a care in the world. Doesn't she realise her baby is missing? I'm beginning to wonder if animals do, in fact, have the same feelings as humans.

2:10 a.m.

I'll never sleep again, obviously.

MONDAY

The phone rang at half past seven in the morning. I must have drifted off.

I collided with Mum and Dad in the kitchen to answer it.

Mum picked it up. "Yes. Yes, I see. Thank you for ringing," she said.

Mum put the phone down and looked at me in that way adults look at you when they have some truly terrible news.

"He's dead!" I wailed. I was crying so loudly I couldn't hear what Mum said at first, but then I realised she was saying: "No, no. He isn't dead. But he's still very poorly indeed and the vet wants to keep him under close observation. She's worried he might have something serious and she's running some tests on him."

I was only a bit relieved by this.

He's DEAD!

4:00 p.m.

Harpo has started looking for Bonzo. She's gone all round the house whimpering. I think I preferred it when she didn't care.

5:00 p.m.

"Tixie."

"Go away, Tomato. I'm busy being sad."

"Got something to tell you," said Tomato.

I looked up. Tomato's round red merry face was tragic and tear-stained. So I gave him a hug. "What is it, Tom Tom?"

"I fink Bonzo has eat my potion."

"WHAT?" I leapt up. "You poured it away, didn't you?"

46

But it turned out Tomato had hidden it under a pile of Dad's planks in the back yard. "What was in it, Tom?" And he burst into tears. "Mum!" I shouted.

10:00 p.m.

Am too tired to write, but must just fill this in.
After Tomato's confession, we phoned the vet and told
her what might be making Bonzo ill.

In Tomato's disgusting week-old, rotting potion was:

- green food colouring
- washing-up liquid
- flour
- a rotten egg (with eggshell)
- mud
- leaves
- pepper
- sugar
- Krispy Popsickles
- muesli
- ink
- bubble bath.

"Thank goodness he didn't use bleach," said Mum.

48

TUESDAY

Mum let me and Tomato go to the hospital with her. When the vet saw us, she rolled her eyes up to the sky. Then she did the nicest thing anyone has ever done in the history of the universe. She laughed. "What a relief," she said. "I was afraid he'd contracted ..." and then she used a Very Extremely long medical word that I can't remember, but that sounded very scary. "Since it hasn't killed him," she said, looking sternly at Tomato, but with a twinkle in her eye, "he should be right as rain in 24 hours."

And she let us take Bonzo home!

49

I can't be cross with Tomato, because I remembered that when I was trying to find a replacement for Anty, I'd taken the ant food out of the fridge to try to tempt the ants. I'm pretty sure I left that bowl outside. Bonzo could just as easily have eaten that ...

Harpo and Bonzo are both snoring peacefully on my bed and I now know the true meaning of happiness.

WELCOME HOME BONZO!!

Amazing

HAPPY!

Best day of my life

Brilliant!!!!

Fantastic

I ♥ BONZO!!

WOW

HOORAY!

YIPPEE

ONE WEEK LATER

(OK, I missed a week. Been too busy cuddling Bonzo, playing football, trumpet and trying to save the world. I bet nobody fills their diary in every day.) Anyway, today we had to present our projects at a special assembly.

Yes! Everyone else's projects were little talks and a few pictures. Our radio show was the best. Everyone laughed, even Warty-Beak smirked a bit. Best of all, the head teacher, Ms Hedake, said it was a "wonderfully imaginative piece of work that shows us how to put ourselves in others' shoes, or perhaps I should say 'paws'," (giggle giggle) "and also how to get a point across in an entertaining way".

We were all going out of our MINDS
Until somebody treated us KIND.
So always remember, whatever you do,
That ANIMALS ARE PEOPLE TOO!

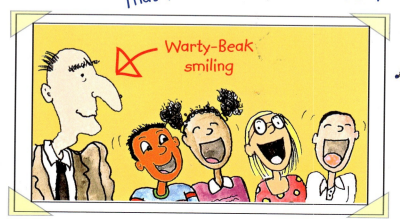

Warty-Beak smiling

51

Still, I've realised, after Bonzo's brush with death, that animals have a right just to be healthy and happy. So now I'm going to concentrate on my new idea. I'm going to write a book called: Trixie's Very Extremely Brilliant Guide to Everything. It'll include my thoughts on animals, football, friends, families, school, music, saving the planet ... but NOT teaching animals to read!

Feed BONZO!

SAVE A SHEEP GO VEGGIE

SAVE THE HEDGEHOG

53

BONZO'S DOGGY DIARY

(translated from doggy talk!)

Monday

Trixie's little brother and his friends are cooking. If I do my best begging act, they might let me try some.

Tuesday

Trixie is playing a new card game with me. The cards taste much better than Tomato's potion and I'm feeling nice and full.

Wednesday

I've got a bit of a tummy ache. Perhaps Trixie's cards didn't agree with me. Come to think of it, she wasn't very pleased that I ate them.

Thursday

I don't feel very well. My tummy feels as if it's got an elephant in it and my chest hurts. But Mum is licking me and that feels nice.

Friday

I feel sick. I am sick. Trixie's being extra nice to me because she knows I'm not very well.

Saturday

Feeling too poorly to write my diary ... *woof, woof.*

Sunday

I've been very sick and I can't breathe properly. Trixie's mum has wrapped me in a blanket. We're in the doggy hospital waiting to see the doctor.

Monday

I slept in a new bed last night ... the doggy doctor is quite strict, but I feel safe with her. *woof, woof.*

Tuesday

I'm better! The doctor gave me something to drink ... and now I'm fine! It must have been something I ate. I'm going home! WOOF! WOOF!

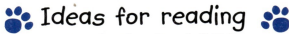

Ideas for reading

Written by Clare Dowdall PhD
Lecturer and Primary Literacy Consultant

Learning objectives: infer writer's perspective from what is written and what is implied; explore how writers use language for comic and dramatic effects; present a spoken argument, sequencing points logically, defending views and making use of persuasive language

Curriculum links: Citizenship: Animals and us, Developing our school grounds

Interest words: ventriloquist, campaigned, fiends, wheezing, severed, collided, confession, contracted

Resources: other diaries, ICT for access to blogs

Getting started

This book can be read over two or more guided reading sessions.

- Ask children to read the title and blurb on the front and back covers of the book. As a group, discuss what children know about diaries and diary writing.

- Encourage children to share their own experiences with diary, blog or profile page writing. Find out: who their pages are written for; what information they include; how they make their pages appealing etc.

Reading and responding

- Focus on the *About Me* section of Trixie's diary (pp3–10). In pairs, ask children to read this section and collect information about Trixie's character (*clever, lively, funny, cheeky* etc.).

- Share ideas about Trixie's character. Ask children to decide whether the author has told the reader this information, or whether the children have inferred it from the text and pictures.

- Read p11 together. Explore how the author has used language to bring Trixie to life and to entertain the reader (conversational tone, mixture of text types and images, repetition of ideas, additional information on sticky notes).